CARTOON NETWORK

SCOOBY-DOO!
AND THE
CARNIVAL CREEPER

Written by
James Gelsey

WORLDWIDE PUBLISHING ™

A
LITTLE APPLE
PAPERBACK

SCHOLASTIC INC.
New York   Toronto   London   Auckland   Sydney
Mexico City   New Delhi   Hong Kong

For Hunter

ISBN 0-439-11346-6

12 11 10 9 8 7 6 5 4   0 1 2 3 4/0

Cover and interior illustrations by Duendes Del Sur.

Printed in the U.S.A.

First Scholastic printing, November 1999

"Here we are, gang," Fred said. "Pops' Big Top Carnival." Fred steered the Mystery Machine into the parking lot. Scooby-Doo was the first one out of the van.

"Roh boy, roh boy," he barked. "Ret's ro!"

"Like, wait for us, Scooby," Shaggy called. He stepped out of the van, followed by Daphne, Velma, and Fred. They all started walking toward the front gate. Scooby kept running ahead of the others.

"What's gotten into you, Scooby-Doo?" Daphne asked.

"Like, he loves carnivals," Shaggy replied.

"He just loves the food at carnivals," Velma said.

"And why not?" Shaggy asked. "You've got your four basic food groups there."

"I know I'm going to be sorry I asked this," Velma said. "But what four basic food groups?"

"Popcorn, peanuts, cotton candy, and snow cones," Shaggy said.

"Reah, reah," Scooby agreed. His big pink tongue swept across his lips.

The gang walked up to the ticket booth. A man with short red hair stood in the booth. He was wearing a red-and-white-striped jacket.

"Welcome to Pops' Big Top Carnival," he said. "I'm Pops Warner, the 'Pops' in the Big Top. Have a great day." He handed Fred the tickets, and the gang walked through the front gate.

"Jinkies," Velma said, pointing. "Look at that amazing Ferris wheel."

The gang looked around and saw the carnival spread out in all directions. The carousel and other rides were straight ahead.

Off to the left, they could see a row of carnival games. Down to the right, they could see a row of brightly colored tents.

Behind them, just inside the front gate, they saw a row of large posters. There was one with a big gray elephant on it. Its head was raised up and its mouth was open.

"Bossie the Laughing Elephant," Fred said, reading the poster. "I wonder how you make an elephant laugh."

"Rickle ris runk?" Scooby asked. He and Shaggy giggled.

"Look at this," Daphne said, pointing to the next poster. It was a picture of a muscular man holding up a car all by himself. "Astoundo, the Strongest Man in the World," Daphne read.

"Jinkies," Velma said. "That *is* astounding."

"That's nothing," Shaggy said. "Right, Scoob?"

"Right!" Scooby barked.

Fred, Daphne, and Velma looked at one another. "What are you two talking about?" Fred said.

"Sure, he can lift a car," Shaggy said. "But can he lift a super-duper, quadruple-decker, Scooby-Doober submarine sandwich and eat it in one bite? Show 'em, Scooby."

Scooby stood up and pretended to make a super-duper, quadruple-decker, Scooby-Doober submarine sandwich. The make-believe sandwich got taller and taller. Scooby pretended to put the last piece of bread on top. He bent over and slipped one paw under the bottom of the invisible sandwich. He put another paw on top of the invisible sandwich. He took a deep breath and then, using all his might, squeezed the enormous pretend sandwich together. He opened his mouth and gobbled it down in one gigantic bite.

"CHOMP! G-u-u-u-u-u-u-lp. Ahhhh-hhhhh." Scooby sat down next to Shaggy and raised his front paws to show off his Scooby muscles.

"Great job, Scooby," Shaggy said. "You could show that Astoundo guy a thing or two about real strength."

"Here's your chance," Velma said. "He's coming this way."

The gang looked up and saw Astoundo walking toward them.

"Yikes!" Shaggy exclaimed. "Like, I didn't mean now!" He and Scooby ducked behind Fred, Daphne, and Velma.

Chapter 2

stoundo, the Strongest Man in the World, walked right past Fred, Daphne, and Velma. He stopped behind the ticket booth and knocked on the door. He was holding a short piece of rope. The door opened and Pops Warner stepped out.

"Do you see this, Pops?" Astoundo said. He shook the piece of rope at Pops. "Someone cut one of the ropes that hold up my tent!"

"When?" Pops asked.

"Just now," the strong man replied. "And I saw the Creeper running away from my tent."

Pops looked concerned. "At least he didn't cut all of the ropes and make your tent collapse," he said. "Don't worry, Astoundo, we'll catch him."

"You'd better," Astoundo said. "If this stuff keeps up, I'm going to leave. And if I leave, this whole carnival will close down. And you wouldn't want that, would you, Pops?"

"Of course not, Astoundo," Pops said.

The strong man turned and walked back to his tent. Fred stepped forward.

"Excuse me, Pops," Fred said. "Is everything all right? We couldn't help but overhear what Astoundo was saying."

"I don't know what to do," Pops said. "Just yesterday, somebody saw the Creeper running out of Bossie's tent. A few minutes later, Bossie was running down the midway, laughing up a storm."

"And you think the Creeper opened Bossie's pen and cut the rope to Astoundo's tent?" Velma asked.

"I don't know what to think," Pops said. "All I know is that if word gets out about these things, we'll be in big trouble."

"Judging from the look of things, I'd say you already are in big trouble," a strange voice said. Everyone turned and saw a tall man wearing a blue plaid suit. He was eating popcorn from a red-and-white striped paper bag. "The crowds are really starting to thin out around here."

"Now see here, Mr. Plenty," Pops said. "I have nothing more to say to you. I'm not selling, so build your mall someplace else. Now, if you don't mind, please leave."

"But I'm a paying customer," the man said, holding out his ticket. He then took a map of the carnival out of his pocket.

"What're you looking for?" Pops asked impatiently.

"Where I can build the food court," the man said. "Remind me to get your popcorn recipe. It's the best I've ever had. Popcorn, anyone?" As he walked away, the man dropped the bag from his hand. Before it could hit the ground, Shaggy and Scooby-Doo dove for the bag and grabbed it.

"Like, no point in wasting perfectly good popcorn," Shaggy said. He and Scooby

munched on the popcorn.

"Who was that?" Daphne asked.

"I don't know," Shaggy whispered to Scooby. "But anyone who wants to build a food court can't be all bad."

"That's J. J. Plenty, a local businessman," Pops said. "He won't take no for an answer. Now, why don't you kids go and have a great afternoon. That's what you're here for." Pops smiled and walked away.

"So what do you think we should do first?" Velma asked.

"Leave!" an old woman said as she walked by the gang. "The exit's that way. It's  time you went home and attended to your studies!"

"Excuse me?" Daphne asked.

"It's carnivals like these that keep children away from their studies," the woman continued. "Someone needs to close this place down. Children need to attend to their studies." The old woman continued on her way.

"Jinkies, what a strange woman," Velma said.

"Imagine, not wanting kids to have any fun," Daphne added.

"Let's forget her and do what Pops asked us to," Fred said. "Let's have a good time. Where do you want to start?"

"Games!" Shaggy said.

"Rides!" Daphne said.

"Shows!" Velma said.

"Food!" Scooby barked.

"Why don't we split up and then

meet at the carousel?" Fred said.

"Sounds good to me," Shaggy said. "C'mon, Scoob, let's go play some games and get some food." Shaggy and Scooby ran off toward the carnival booths.

"Now don't you two get into any trouble!" Daphne called after them.

"Like, don't worry about us!" Shaggy called back. "What kind of trouble can we get into at a carnival?"

"I'm afraid to find out," Velma said.

$\mathcal{S}$haggy and Scooby walked down the long row of carnival games. Shaggy was eating a snow cone. Scooby had some cotton candy.

"Step right up and try your luck!" a man yelled. "All it takes is a cool head and a keen eye. How about you?" Shaggy and Scooby stopped and looked around.

"Like, do you think he's talking to us?" Shaggy said.

"That's right, I'm talking to you," a man from one of the game booths shouted. "You look like a couple of winners. Come on over!"

14

Shaggy and Scooby shrugged and walked over to the booth.

"Pleased to meet you," the man said. "Stitch Morgan's the name, baseball's the game. The rules are simple. All you have to do is knock those three milk bottles down with this here baseball. Piece of cake, especially for someone with your athletic build."

"Me? Athletic build?" Shaggy said. "Man, you must need glasses."

"Nope, they're not glasses," Stitch said. "They're milk bottles. Like I said. So give it a try. Three throws for a dollar."

"Why not?" Shaggy said. "Here, Scooby, hold my snow cone." Shaggy gave Stitch a dollar bill. Stitch placed three baseballs on the counter in front of Shaggy. Shaggy picked up a baseball. He looked at the three white milk bottles stacked in a pyramid.

"Scoob, this is gonna be easy," Shaggy said. Shaggy reached his arm back and then threw a ball at the milk bottles.

Whoosh! Shaggy missed.

"That was mighty close," Stitch said. "Two more tries. You can do it, pal. I know you can."

"I was just warming up that time," Shaggy said. "This one's for real." Shaggy grabbed another baseball. He carefully lined himself up with the milk bottles.

"It's really all physics, Scooby," Shaggy said. "Just throw the ball in the right direction and gravity does the rest. Watch." Shaggy reached back and threw the ball right at the milk bottles.

Whoosh!

"Now that's quite a curveball you've got there, pal," Stitch said. "Can't say I've ever seen a ball make a left turn in midair like that. One more try."

"That's it. I'm going to use my special Shaggy Fastball. Those milk bottles will never know what hit them."

Shaggy picked up a baseball. He gripped it in his right hand. He leaned over a bit

and squinted both his eyes. Shaggy stood up, reached his right arm behind him, closed his eyes, and threw the ball with all his might.

Crash!

"I did it! I did it!" Shaggy exclaimed, his eyes still closed. "Didn't I?"

Shaggy opened one eye and looked at the ground. He saw the three milk bottles on the floor. But when he looked up to see the table, he saw the Creeper standing there instead. He was hunched over and he wore a green suit. And he was holding the baseball!

"Arrrrrrrrrrrr," the Creeper growled.

"Zoinks!" Shaggy cried.

"Rikes!" Scooby barked.

Scooby and Shaggy ducked and covered their heads.

The people at the other games started screaming and running away. The Creeper jumped over the railing and ran down the midway. He disappeared into one of the tents.

Shaggy and Scooby slowly raised their heads and looked around.

Stitch came out from under the table. "That's one creepy-looking character," he said.

"Wait'll the others hear about this,"

Shaggy said. He and Scooby got up to go.

"Hold on there, partner," Stitch said. "Don't forget your prize."

"Like, for what?" Shaggy asked.

"Well, those milk bottles didn't just fall onto the floor by themselves," Stitch answered. "So here's your prize."

Stitch handed Shaggy a great big stuffed teddy bear. It was blue with an orange bow tie.

"Thanks, Stitch," Shaggy said.

When Scooby saw the bear, he started wagging his tail.

"Awww," Scooby sighed. "Reddy rear."

Shaggy put the bear on Scooby's back. "All right, Scooby, you can have him," Shaggy said. "Now, let's go find the others."

Chapter 4

S haggy and Scooby walked up to the rest of the gang at the carousel.

"Like, you're not going to believe what just happened to us," Shaggy said.

Daphne looked at the teddy bear on Scooby's back. "Let me guess," she said. "You two won this teddy bear."

"Well, yeah," Shaggy said, "but we also saw the Creeper!"

"The Creeper?" Velma exclaimed.

"Where?" Daphne asked.

"Back at the games," Shaggy said. "One minute, I'm throwing a baseball, the next

20

minute, like, there's this Creeper dude about to jump on our heads."

"So what happened?" Fred asked.

"He ran right past us and down the midway," Shaggy said. "Then we lost him."

The attendant at the carousel walked over to the gang.

"Excuse me, would you like to ride the carousel?" she asked. "I have to run it anyway so people can hear the music all over the carnival. It will be a special ride just for you."

"Won't the carnival owner get mad?" Daphne asked.

"He can't get mad at his own daughter,"

the attendant said. "I'm Maisy Warner." She took off her cap, revealing a head of red hair.

"She's Pops' daughter, all right," Shaggy said.

"We're starting to worry about being able to keep the carnival open," Maisy said. "The place has really started emptying out. I think it's because word is getting out about the mysterious Creeper."

"Or that mean old woman who hates fun," Shaggy said.

"That's Mrs. Krumb," Maisy said. "She's here all the time. She's a little strange, but no one really takes her seriously."

"Well, Pops did ask us to have a good time," Fred said. "But I don't think we could take a ride after eating so much popcorn."

"Maybe you can't, Freddo," Shaggy said, "but Scooby-Doo can."

Everyone turned and saw that Scooby-Doo was already seated on one of the horses.

"One passenger's better than no passengers," Maisy said. She walked toward the center of the carousel. She opened a door and reached inside. She pulled a lever, and the carousel slowly started moving. Loud organ music began playing. The gang watched.

"Groooovy!" Shaggy yelled.

"Look at Scooby go!" Daphne exclaimed.

"Ree-hah," Scooby barked from his horse on the carousel.

The carousel was going full blast when everyone heard a scream. They looked at the center of the carousel. The gang saw Maisy standing next to the control panel.

"The Creeper! The Creeper!" she yelled.

Suddenly, the Creeper jumped out from behind one of the horses.

"*Arrrrrrrrrr!*" he moaned at them.

"Raggy! Relp!" Scooby barked.

"Quick, Maisy, stop the ride!" Fred yelled.

Maisy raised the control lever. As the carousel slowed down, the Creeper jumped off and ran into the carnival.

"So there really is a Creeper," Velma said.

Scooby jumped off the carousel and into Shaggy's arms. Pops ran over to them.

"Is everything all right?" he asked.

"We're fine, Pops," Maisy said. "But that Creeper has got to go."

"I know, Maisy," Pops

said. "But I don't know what to do."

Fred, Velma, and Daphne all looked at one another and nodded.

"Excuse us a minute, Pops," Fred said. The whole gang huddled together. Then they all turned back to face Pops.

"We'll get to the bottom of this," Fred said. "And take care of the Creeper."

Chapter 5

"Let's split up to look for clues," Fred said.
"Great idea, Fred," Velma said. "Shaggy, Scooby, and I will check around Bossie's tent."

"And Fred and I will look around Astoundo's tent," Daphne said.

"We'll meet back here when we're done," Fred said. Fred and Daphne walked off toward Astoundo's tent.

Velma, Shaggy, and Scooby walked in the other direction. As they neared a big green-and-yellow tent, Velma pointed to a banner that said BOSSIE THE LAUGHING ELEPHANT.

"This must be the place," Shaggy said. As they were about to go into the tent, a loud sound came from inside.

"Man, what is that noise?" Shaggy said.

"It sounds like someone's playing a broken trumpet," Velma said.

"Or squeezing a goose," Shaggy added.

Scooby couldn't take the noise any longer. He pulled his teddy bear next to his right ear. He covered his left ear with one paw and the teddy bear's ear with his other paw.

A moment later, the sound stopped and the three of them walked into the tent. There they saw a large fenced area, and inside stood a big gray elephant.

27

"That must be Bossie," Velma said. "I'll bet that the sound we heard was her laughing."

"If that was Bossie's laugh," Shaggy whispered to Scooby, "remind me not to tell her any jokes."

Scooby giggled at Shaggy's remark. Bossie's ears perked up. Bossie turned her head in Scooby's direction and raised her trunk.

"Eeeeeee-ahahahahahahahahahahahah!"

"Oh, no, she's at it again!" Shaggy said. "This is no laughing matter."

Shaggy, Velma, and Scooby all covered their ears. Bossie stopped laughing and went back to eating her hay.

"Hmmmm," Velma said. "I have a hunch that Bossie laughs when she hears other people laugh. So whatever you do, don't laugh." Velma walked toward Bossie's pen and started looking around. "You two go around the other side."

Shaggy and Scooby went the opposite way around Bossie's pen.

"Hey, Scooby," Shaggy whispered. "Do you know the difference between an elephant and an aspirin?"

"Ruh-uh," Scooby said, shaking his head.

"Then I'm never sending you to the store for aspirin," Shaggy said, smiling.

"Ree-hee." Scooby started laughing. Shaggy quickly put his hand over Scooby's mouth.

"You'd better not, Scoob," Shaggy warned. "Unless you want another earful of that elephant's laughter." But it was too late. Bossie raised her trunk and was getting ready to laugh. "Look out," Shaggy called. "She's gonna blow!"

"Rikes!" Scooby barked. Scooby jumped into Shaggy's arms and covered his ears. As he jumped, he dropped his teddy bear on the ground. Before Bossie could get any sound out, she noticed the teddy bear. She lowered her head and slowly walked over toward it. Shaggy and Scooby relaxed as Bossie gazed at the teddy bear through the fence. Then Bossie looked up at Scooby-Doo and raised her trunk again. Shaggy and Scooby braced themselves for another blast.

"She's not going to laugh," Velma said, walking over. "I think she wants the teddy bear."

"Like, I knew that," Shaggy said.

Scooby-Doo picked up the bear and held it out to Bossie. Bossie nodded eagerly.

"Rere," Scooby barked. He tossed the teddy bear over the fence and into the pen. As Bossie ran over to get it, the ground shook under each step. She picked up the teddy bear and cradled it in her trunk.

"That was very nice of you, Scooby," Velma said. "I'd say this has been a very successful visit. Scooby made a friend, and I found a clue."

"What did you find, Velma?" Shaggy asked.

"A very interesting piece of paper right beside the gate to Bossie's pen," she replied. "Let's go meet the others and see what they found."

They were about to leave when Bossie gave a short laugh. She waved her trunk at Scooby and something flew through the air.

Scooby sniffed the air and then caught the object in his mouth. He chewed happily.

"Reanuts!" Scooby barked. "Ranks, Rossie!"

"Speaking of peanuts, I'm a little hungry myself," Shaggy said. "Velma, is it okay if we stop for a quick snack on our way back?"

"I want to see what Fred and Daphne found," Velma answered. "You two get something and meet us back at the carousel. But don't take too long."

"We'll be there before you know it," Shaggy said. "You can count on us."

Chapter 6

Shaggy and Scooby walked down the midway and passed lots of snack stands. As they walked, Shaggy read the signs.

"So, what'll it be, pal of mine?" Shaggy asked Scooby. "Cotton candy? Peanuts? Popcorn? Snow cone? Pizza? Funnel cake?" They both stopped, looked at each other, and nodded.

"Pizza!" they sang together. Shaggy and Scooby turned to walk over to the pizza stand. As they did, they passed a donuts shack. Out front was the biggest donut they had ever seen.

"Man, that donut's almost as big as my appetite!" Shaggy said.

Scooby sat down and stared at the donut. He licked his lips. Then Shaggy and Scooby heard a moan.

"Please tell me that was your stomach, Scoob," Shaggy whimpered.

"Nope!" Scooby said.

Suddenly, the Creeper jumped through the center of the donut!

"Arrrrrrrrrrr!" the Creeper growled.

"Rikes!" Scooby barked.

"Zoinks!" Shaggy exclaimed.

Shaggy and Scooby turned and ran down the midway. The Creeper was right behind them. Shaggy and Scooby weaved around the snack stands and garbage cans, but the Creeper stayed close behind.

"In here, Scoob!" Shaggy called. He and Scooby ran through a bright yellow door. The Creeper followed them inside. They were all in the Fun House!

Inside, Shaggy and Scooby ran up a metal staircase. At the top, they walked carefully across a skinny bridge made entirely out of thick rope. Beneath the bridge was a giant pit filled with colored balls.

"Keep moving, Scooby," Shaggy said. "The Creeper is still behind us."

The bridge led to a room that was tilted on its side. The things that were supposed to be on the floor were on the wall!

"Now I know what a fly feels like,"

Shaggy said as he walked across the room. Then, Shaggy and Scooby walked through a series of swinging doors that got smaller and smaller. On the other side of the last door they found themselves in a hall of mirrors.

One of the mirrors made Shaggy look extremely tall and skinny. Another made Scooby look really short and stumpy. They couldn't help but laugh.

"Hey, Scooby!" Shaggy called. "Look at me. I'm as tall as a telephone pole."

"Raggy!" Scooby barked. "Rook at me. I'm a hot dog!"

Shaggy and Scooby were laughing so hard they didn't see the Creeper come into the room behind them. The Creeper raised his arms and moaned at them. Shaggy and Scooby took one look and laughed even harder. The Creeper was standing in front of a mirror that made him look wiggly, like a piece of spaghetti. The Creeper looked in the mirror and saw himself.

"Ha-ha-ha-ha-ha-ha-ha!" The Creeper broke out in laughter, too. While the Creeper was laughing, Shaggy and Scooby inched toward the doorway. They quickly ran through it and found themselves standing in front of a spinning tunnel.

"Come on, Scooby," Shaggy said. "We have to go through it in order to get out of here."

"Ruh-uh," Scooby said, shaking his head.

The Creeper walked through the doorway behind them and moaned.

"The Creeper!" Shaggy yelled. He grabbed Scooby and the two of them ran into the spinning tunnel.

The Creeper followed them in and grabbed Scooby's tail. Scooby lost his balance and fell down. Then the Creeper fell down, too, letting go of Scooby. Scooby and the Creeper bounced off the sides of the tunnel as it spun around and around.

Shaggy made it out of the tunnel first.

"Crawl out, Scooby," Shaggy called back. "You can do it!"

Scooby crawled out. He and Shaggy looked back and saw the Creeper trapped in the tunnel, spinning around and around. A piece of paper flew out of the tunnel. It landed on the ground and opened up.

"Look, it's a map of the carnival," Shaggy said. "This'll help us find our way back to meet the others."

"Ret's ro!" Scooby barked.

Chapter 7

Back at the carousel, Fred, Daphne, and Velma were comparing notes. Maisy was listening in.

"Did you find anything interesting around Astoundo's tent?" Velma asked the others.

"Not really," Fred said. "It looked like someone had already repaired the cut rope. Everything else seemed pretty ordinary."

"Except for all that trash," Daphne said.

"What kind of trash?" Velma asked.

"We found a huge pile of red-and-white popcorn bags," Daphne replied.

"Jinkies," Velma said.

"What did you find, Velma?" Fred asked.

"I found this by the gate to Bossie's pen," Velma said. She held out a crumpled-up red paper bag.

"Looks like our Creeper likes popcorn," Daphne said.

Just then, Shaggy and Scooby ran up to the carousel. They were out of breath.

"What happened to you two?" Fred asked.

"Like, the Creeper was after us," Shaggy explained. "We were on our way to get a snack and he chased us into the Fun House. And he almost got Scooby-Doo, too."

"Reah!" Scooby barked, nodding. "Rike ris." Scooby pretended to run. Then he reached back and grabbed his tail with one of his paws. Then, pretending he was the Creeper, Scooby gave his tail a hard tug. Scooby fell to the ground and then started rolling around.

"We left him in the Fun House," Shaggy explained. "Man, he was tumbling around like socks in a clothes dryer."

He and Scooby giggled.

"Now, I don't know about you guys," Shaggy continued, "but Scooby and I never got to have our snack, so we're going to get some food." Shaggy took a folded piece of paper from his pocket and opened it up. Scooby looked over his shoulder.

"Hey, watch it, Scooby," Shaggy said. "Your hot Scooby breath is curling the paper."

Velma came over and looked at the map. "Where did you get this?" she asked.

"I found it outside the Fun House," Shaggy replied. "It must've fallen out of the Creeper's pocket."

"Let me see," Fred said. Shaggy handed Fred the paper.

"Hmm," Velma said. "I have a hunch that the Creeper has made his last bit of mischief around here."

"I think you're right, Velma," Fred said, nodding. "Gang, it's time to set a trap." Fred turned to Daphne and Maisy. "You two go find Pops and ask him to meet us at the Ferris wheel."

"No problem," Daphne said.

"Velma and I will be stationed there, waiting for the Creeper," Fred continued. "We'll take care of everything there."

"And that's where you two come in," Velma said to Shaggy and Scooby.

"Huh?" Scooby asked.

"You two will lure the Creeper to the Ferris wheel," Velma said.

"Like, how come we get stuck with the Creeper?" Shaggy asked.

"Because he already knows you," Daphne answered. "And I'm sure he's pretty upset about your leaving him in the Fun House."

"Ro way!" Scooby barked.

"Come on, Scooby," Fred said.

Scooby sat down with his paws crossed.

"Will you do it for a Scooby Snack?" Velma asked.

"Ruh-uh," Scooby said.

"Will you do it for two Scooby Snacks?" Daphne asked.

Scooby turned his head and looked away.

"How about for two Scooby Snacks and all the cotton candy, popcorn, and snow cones you can eat?" Maisy offered.

Scooby's eyes lit up and a big smile crossed his face.

"Rokay!" he barked, wagging his tail.

Velma took two Scooby Snacks out of her pocket and tossed them into the air, one at a time. Scooby jumped up and gobbled up each one in midair.

"Hey, that's pretty good, Scooby," Maisy said. "You know, with a little practice, you could be a real carnival show dog."

"Awww," Scooby said, blushing a little.

"We're running out of time, gang," Fred said. "So let's get to work."

Chapter 8

Daphne and Maisy walked off toward the front gate to find Pops. Fred and Velma turned and headed for the Ferris wheel. Shaggy and Scooby watched the others walk away.

"Hey, Scoob," Shaggy said. "What do you say we play a quick game on the midway? I know I can knock those milk bottles down again."

"Rokay," Scooby said. The two of them walked back toward the midway. They stopped off for a bag of popcorn first.

As Shaggy ate some popcorn, he realized that most of the games were closed. When he saw Stitch Morgan coming toward them, he called out, "Like, what's going on, Stitch?"

"Pops decided to close early today," Stitch replied. "You know, with all the excitement about that Creeper. But come back again." Stitch continued on his way.

"If the carnival is closing, that means we're going to be here, like, all alone with the Creeper," Shaggy said.

Suddenly, it became very quiet. Then they heard someone moaning in the distance.

"Oh, no," Shaggy whimpered. "Here we go again."

The Creeper jumped out from behind one of the closed-up booths. "Arrrrrrrrr!" he screamed at Shaggy and Scooby.

"Rikes!" Scooby yelped.

"Like, let's hightail it out of here, Scooby," Shaggy said.

Shaggy and Scooby turned and ran. The

Creeper started running after them. They ran past the games and snack stands. They ran past the carousel. They ran past the sideshow tents.

"Like, (*gasp*), where's the (*gasp*), Ferris wheel?" Shaggy yelled as he ran.

"Ri don't know," Scooby replied.

They saw Bossie's green-and-yellow tent. Shaggy and Scooby ran inside. The Creeper followed closely behind them. Bossie was in her pen, cradling the teddy bear in her trunk. She watched the Creeper chase Shaggy and Scooby around her pen and out the other side of the tent. The Ferris wheel was just

ahead, and Shaggy and Scooby ran toward it.

"Like, Fred, help!" Shaggy called.

Fred and Velma stepped out from the control booth at the base of the Ferris wheel.

"In here!" they called. Shaggy ran toward the booth, but Scooby didn't hear Fred. He was too busy looking over his shoulder at the Creeper, who was getting closer. The Creeper was just about to grab Scooby when Scooby ran into one of the cars on the Ferris wheel. He closed the door behind him.

"Quick, start it up!" Shaggy yelled. "The Creeper's going to get Scooby!"

Inside the booth, Pops hit the switch and the Ferris wheel started moving. Scooby was safe inside his car. He poked his head out and saw the Creeper jump into another car.

Up, up, up went Scooby and the Creeper. When the Creeper's car was near the top, Pops hit the emergency brake and stopped the ride.

"We caught the Creeper!" Maisy yelled with delight.

"And Scooby-Doo," Velma added.

"Relp!" Scooby yelled.

"We have to get him down," Shaggy said.

Pops released the brake. "Something's wrong," he said. "I can't restart the Ferris wheel."

"So what'll we do?" Daphne asked.

"Wait for the police," Pops said. "Scooby should be fine. The cars on the Ferris wheel are very safe. Besides, the Creeper isn't going anywhere."

"You may have spoken too soon, Pops,"

Fred said. He pointed to the top of the Ferris wheel. "Look!"

Everyone looked up. The Creeper was crawling out of his car. He started climbing very slowly down the frame of the Ferris wheel.

"He's trying to get to Scooby-Doo!" Daphne exclaimed.

"Don't worry, buddy," Shaggy called. "We'll save you!"

"How?" Velma asked.

"Like, I was hoping you'd think of something," Shaggy said.

Just then, everyone felt the ground shake.

"Was that an earthquake?" Maisy said.

"No, an elephant quake!" Shaggy replied. Everyone turned and saw Bossie running toward the Ferris wheel. With each step, the ground shook.

"If the Creeper's here, who let Bossie out of her pen?" Pops asked.

"I did," Stitch Morgan said. He came running up behind Bossie. "On my way out, I heard a ruckus coming from Bossie's tent. She looked like she was going to bust down the fence around her pen, so I figured I'd better let her out."

"Relp! Raggy!" Scooby barked from the Ferris wheel. The Creeper was getting closer.

Bossie walked to the Ferris wheel and looked up at Scooby. Bossie stood up on her rear legs. Then she raised her head and extended her trunk as far as it would go. It just reached the bottom of Scooby's car.

"Rere roes!" Scooby said. He closed his eyes and slid down to her trunk.

"Hooray!" everyone cried.

Scooby opened his eyes. He looked up and saw the Creeper climbing back inside the Ferris wheel car. The Creeper was waving his hands angrily and growling.

Scooby was safe, and the Creeper was trapped.

Chapter 9

A little while later, Pops managed to reset the Ferris wheel and start it up again. The police arrived as the car with the Creeper reached the bottom. Pops stopped the ride and two policemen helped the Creeper out of the car.

"Now, let's see who this Creeper really is," Pops said. He reached over and pulled off the Creeper's mask.

"Astoundo!" Pops exclaimed. "You're the Creeper?"

"Just as we suspected," Velma said.

"But how did you know?" Maisy asked.

"If anyone, I thought for sure it was J. J. Plenty."

"So did we at first," Fred replied. "After all, Mr. Plenty made no secret of wanting to close down the carnival so he could build his shopping mall here."

"That, plus the popcorn bag we found at Bossie's pen suggested that the Creeper loved popcorn," Velma said. "Just like Mr. Plenty."

"We also found a big pile of red-and-white bags outside Astoundo's tent," Daphne added.

"But the thing that really tipped us off was the map Shaggy and Scooby got from the Creeper," Velma said. Velma took the map from her pocket and unfolded it. It was a map of the carnival.

"There are circles around Bossie's pen and the carousel," Maisy said as she looked at the map. "Those are the places where the Creeper was."

"There is no circle around Astoundo's tent," Velma said.

"The Creeper never circled Astoundo's tent because he never really did anything there," Fred said.

"That's why it looked to us like the rope holding up his tent was already fixed," Daphne added. "It was never cut in the first place."

"Astoundo made up the whole thing so you wouldn't suspect him," Velma added.

"But what about Mrs. Krumb?" Maisy asked. "Did you suspect her at all?"

"Not really," Fred said. "She may not have liked the carnival, but she couldn't move as fast as the Creeper did."

"Boy, you kids are something else," Pops

said. "As for you, Astoundo, why did you do all those things?"

"Because I was tired of getting second billing to an elephant," Astoundo replied. "I was going to make a deal with that real estate guy. He could build his mall and make me the star attraction."

"Hmmm, what an interesting idea," J. J. Plenty said.

"How did you get in here?" Pops asked. "I closed the carnival an hour ago."

"I actually never left," J. J. Plenty said. "I still have my ticket, see? And I have a new proposition for you. What do you say we go into business together?"

"What do you mean?" Pops asked.

"I'll build my mall, but we'll attach your carnival to it," J. J. said. "Imagine the possibilities."

"Hey, that's my idea!" Astoundo shouted as the police dragged him away. "Blast those kids and their meddling dog!"

"Mr. Plenty, you may be onto something," Pops said with a smile. Then he turned to the gang.

"Thank you all so much. You truly helped save my carnival. As a token of my appreciation, you can come to the carnival free of charge anytime you wish. And please don't forget to bring your wonderful dog."

"Speaking of our wonderful dog," Daphne said, "has anyone seen Scooby?"

"No, but I have a hunch where we'll find him," Velma said. Everyone walked back to Bossie's tent. Inside they found Scooby and the teddy bear perched atop Bossie's head. Bossie picked up some popcorn with her trunk and tossed it into the air. Scooby jumped up and gobbled it down.

"Hey, what a great act for the carnival!" Pops exclaimed.

"That's no act," Shaggy said. "That's our Scooby-Doo!"

"Scooby-Dooby-Doo!" Scooby barked happily.

About the Author

As a boy, James Gelsey used to run home from school to watch the Scooby-Doo cartoons on television (only after finishing his homework). Today, he still enjoys watching them with his wife and daughter. He also has a real dog named Scooby who loves nothing more than a good Scooby Snack!